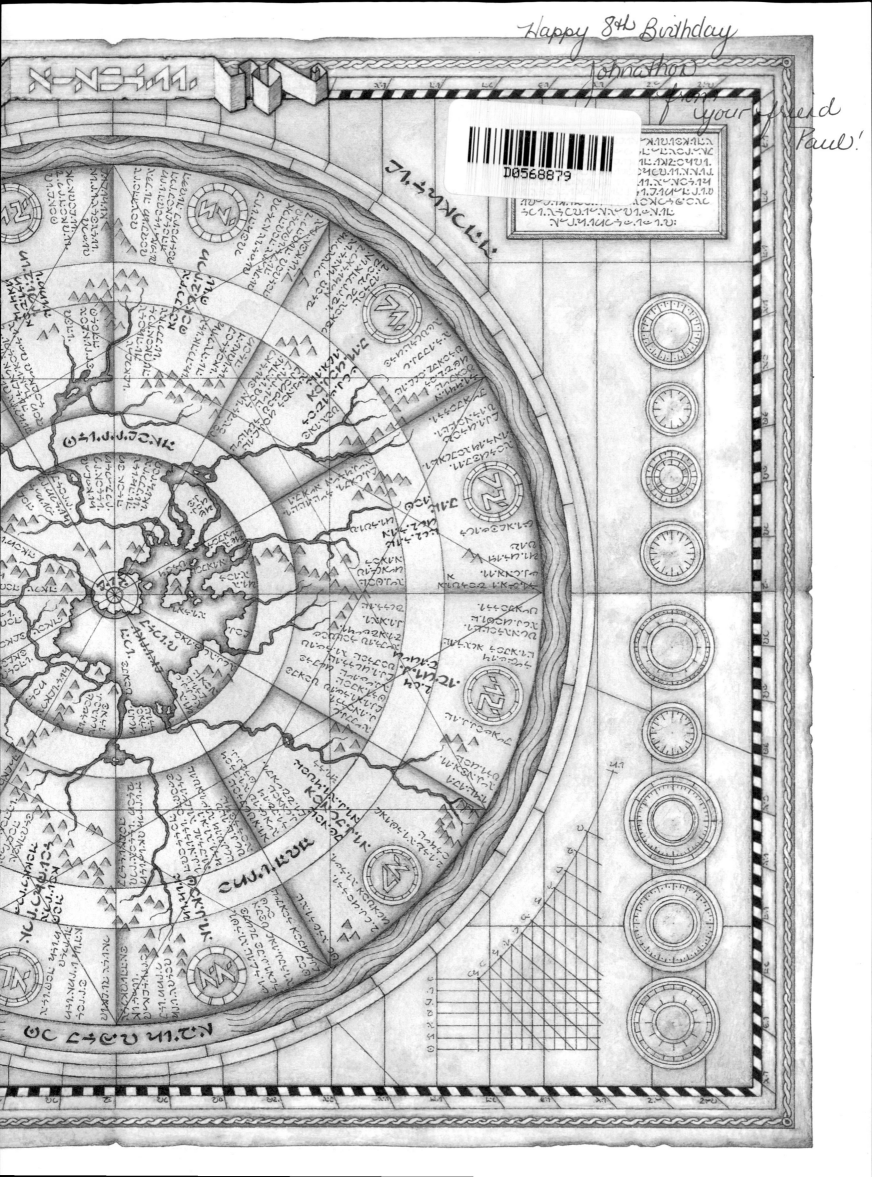

The Quest for the Malbigon

FAR AWAY, BEYOND sea and swamp, desert and perilous mountain range, lies a forgotten and fertile land: the Three Counties. Here live the Gibblins, an oppressed people held firmly in check by a ruthless dictator, Lord Mulciber. Outwardly compliant, they long for the return of the old ways and in particular for the return of their usurped king, but this can never be unless a legendary gemstone—the Malbigon— is restored to its rightful place, on the cover of the book that bears its name.

Some say that the secret of the Malbigon is passed down from generation to generation, and that clues to its whereabouts abound if the seeker is truly acquainted with Gibblin ways. But that, dear traveler, is no easy task. The inhabitants of the Three Counties are not easy to locate, and they have their own customs, alphabet and calendar, and their own myths and legends.

This book provides the essential introduction to the region and its people, and is an indispensable aid for those who wish to join the quest for the Malbigon. Study the maps to get your bearings. Learn the alphabet so that you can decipher and transcribe the Gibblin language. Seek to understand the calendar and consider its implications. And read Caleb Beldragon's chronicle carefully, for perhaps you will be the one to restore the Malbigon and so release the Gibblins to reclaim their heritage.

For Patrick and Miles

Published by Turner Publishing, Inc.
A Subsidiary of Turner Broadcasting System, Inc.
1050 Techwood Drive, N.W., Atlanta, Georgia 30318

ISBN 1-57036-066-9

Distributed by Andrews and McMeel   A Universal Press Syndicate Company
4900 Main Street, Kansas City, Missouri 64112

First published in Great Britain by William Heinemann Limited, an imprint of Reed International Books Limited
First US Edition
10 9 8 7 6 5 4 3 2 1

Printed in China

On previous page: Map of Fumoria, showing the State of Diz and the twelve surrounding Domains of the Fu'athan.

Caleb Beldragon's
CHRONICLE OF THE
THREE COUNTIES

Paul Warren

Turner Publishing, Inc.

ATLANTA

Fumoria, the Malbigon, and the Three Counties

When darkness falls and shadows reign,
With dusky wings o'er his domain,
Or spread across the sunless sea,
To where the dismal breakers roar,
That beat upon some stony shore;
He bids them all,
With heart misshaped:
Come! Obey!—There's no escape!

FROM THE *MALBIGON*

Welcome! May I introduce myself? Caleb Beldragon, at your service, and I offer to be your guide in this forgotten land. You who would travel to the Three Counties, I would first acquaint with other things. You should know that the land of Fumoria once was ruled by a good king who was overthrown by his wicked brother. Afterward, all mention of the king was forbidden so that eventually even his name was forgotten. From time beyond memory, Fumoria has been a shadowland ruled by Lord Mulciber the Deathless, who sits upon the throne like a bloated poisonous spider. But though we know nothing of Mulciber's rise to power, legend has it that one day the good king will rule again.

Next, you should know some geography. At Fumoria's heart lies Diz, the capital city. Extending out from Diz are the Domains of Fumoria, lands granted to twelve aristocratic families known as the *Fu'athan*, or Chosen Ones. The *Malbigon*, a magic book said once to have belonged to the good king and now in the keeping of the jealous Lord Mulciber, describes the Domains as "blighted by deserts, volcanoes, and swamps, where once great cities have fallen to ruin." It also tells of a mysterious distant region, lush and green, that lies on the southern borders of the Domain of Maldemon.

The ancient book known as the Malbigon *derives its name from the great central gemstone that once adorned its cover. The book contains maps, spells, and much valuable information concerning the realm of Fumoria. Though many of its pages are missing, the great gem, if found, would restore the book's magical power. Mulciber seeks this stone above all other things.*

The border of this temperate land faces the Domain of Maldemon over a distance of some twenty-five leagues, from the granite ridges of the Distant Hills in the west to the high walls of the eastern Bluffs. To reach it you must follow the river for three days and nights, then take the ancient road that skirts the Dimmocks, rejoining the river where it plunges between the cliffs of Badland Gap. It is an arduous path, and you will need a stick and stout boots, but, excepting a climb over the sheer walls of the northern hills, it is the only route leading to where, at last, the Three Counties greet the weary traveler.

In olden days, the area known as the Three Counties was popular among the Fu'athan and other highborn families for its forests filled with abundant game, and for a while the region was known as the Chase of Mulciber, but over the years it has fallen out of favor, becoming once more a backwater of market towns and neglected hamlets.

But things in this world are seldom as they seem, and the Three Counties hide many secrets that are revealed only to an expert eye.

Caleb Beldragon, chronicler of the Three Counties.

Throughout the Three Counties, symbols like these are found carved or painted on trees, stones, buildings, bridges, and many artifacts. Some are of great antiquity. The Malbigon *is silent on their meaning, for the pages concerning them are missing.*

Ids, Urgs, and Gibblins

Brave lads are we
Who roamed the hills of Grobbly Bor
To flee the tyrant's lashes,
For fifty days and fifty nights
And nought to eat but ashes.
URG LEGEND

Ids always wear hats
to hide the unsightly lumps
on their heads.

There once were people living in the Three Counties whose origins were rooted in the beginning of time. They have long since vanished, so this history is concerned with the comings and goings of folk here over the past six thousand years. This era is divided into three main periods called the Treglaths, and from the second—or as some call it, the Fu'ath Period—a few highborn families still remain. The rest of the population is divided into three groups. Let me introduce them.

First, the Ids. It is true to say that these sour-faced creatures consider themselves superior to everyone else. They first arrived in the Three Counties as advisors to the aristocratic Fu'athan. Now the bony brutes control the local authorities and the judiciary. Ids never relax and are constantly irritable, so when dealing with them, beware! They are not to be trifled with.

Next, the Urgs. These ugly, restless creatures roam the countryside on the lookout for mischief and are best described as a species of goblin whose main attributes are laziness and greed. They are loud-mouthed, cowardly, uncouth, and cruel—and that's just among themselves! Many join the militia or become bodyguards or bailiffs.

The males outnumber females by at least four to one, but lady Urgs are no shrinking violets, for they are able to draw upon their considerable cantankerousness—not to mention their great physical strength—to give their menfolk as good as they get.

No Urg journeys far without
his money belt, hoping to fill
it on his travels–preferably
with someone else's gold!

They, too, are definitely to be avoided on moonless nights in Darkling Wood.

Lastly, the Gibblins. Sneering Ids and bullying Urgs may consider them country bumpkins and call them drones, but thankfully, Gibblins are the most numerous in the Three Counties. They are cheerful and easygoing, sharp-eyed, and nimble-fingered, with a natural affinity for the land. According to their own stories, they were a wandering tribe before they settled in the region, and long before the rule of Mulciber, there were three recognizable Gibblin types: Halstocks, Fadocs, and Poggs. Though settlement has mingled their blood, they have kept many of their original characteristics, and still can be told apart by the number of points on their ears.

Halstocks have three points, and tend to be taller and stouter, with large feet. They have a keen understanding of plants and are expert gardeners. Fadocs are more adventurous and claim to have been the first Gibblins to cross Badland Gap. They have great skill in handicrafts and are good at inventing things. They love rivers and hills, and most Fadoc families live east of the River Scumcrust, around the Blackdoom Hills. Their ears are two-pointed. Poggs are not often encountered, having retained much of the wandering spirit of their ancestors. They tend to be solitary and love to observe the ways of creatures in the wild. Of old it was said that Poggs could even talk to animals. Their ears have one point.

Halstock ears are three-pointed. Fadoc ears have two points. Pogg ears have one point.

I should also mention the hermits who are sometimes found in out-of-the-way places. I myself have never met one, and little is known of them, though they are said to be great mapmakers. They can be mistaken for wizards, whom no one has ever seen but who are rumored to exist in an extensive secret brotherhood.

Muffin Pigdoom, age eight, is a Halstock Gibblin. So is his cousin, Brassica.

Myths and Legends

Studs the Goblin swore a feud
Against the hairy savage
That marched into his chieftain's camp
To pillage and to ravage.
TRADITIONAL URG SONG

The origins of Gibblins and Urgs lie far back in the mists of time, long before their settling in the Three Counties. Gibblins call this lost era the Golden Age. But whereas their legends recall the time before the fall of the good king, the Urgs' tales deal mainly with the Age of Mulciber, when Fumoria passed into shadow. Of course, Ids, being the official record keepers of Fumoria, consider all such "fairy tales" beneath them. So let's leave them to scratch among their dusty records, while we delve into the magic realms of myth and legend.

Urgs have no written history, but, when Urgs get together, they

love to sing songs and tell stories about their fearsome ancestors. Sometimes the more imaginative Urgs add ballads about their own glorious deeds, usually make-believe accounts of daring exploits in distant lands.

Ever popular is the Urg creation myth known as *The Cauldron of Mulciber*, which tells how Lord Mulciber slew Roroc, the fish-guardian of the Great Inland Sea. The tyrant then flung Roroc's body into a pot to make a fish stew, and from the dregs he conjured up an army of Urg slaves to serve him.

Another story tells how, later, when many Urgs plotted to flee from Mulciber's dominion, they were betrayed by one of their own kind—a mysterious traitor known as the Nameless One. Ever since, he has been blamed whenever misfortune occurs, and to this day Urgs wear charms inscribed with his mark. These charms to the Nameless One are supposed to ward off bad luck.

The earlier arrival of the Gibblins in the Three Counties was formally chronicled, but in the year 1271 of the Second Treglath, Mulciber ordered all books to be burned. Overnight, the Gibblins' *Codex of the Ages* disappeared from the library at Scotty Codfield. Many believe that the *Codex* was hidden and is still being compiled secretly. Whatever the truth, a rich tradition of stories has passed down by word of mouth.

The Gibblin creation myth tells of a giant called Golmeth, who was the son of the Mother of All Things. "Golmeth made the earth and the stars, and his tears filled the Great Inland Sea. His voice was thunder, and his breath was the wind. When he laughed, the weather was fair; if he was sad, clouds filled the sky. When Golmeth died, his body made the four quarters of Fumoria, and his eyes became the sun and the moon. Elmeth and Noth, his son and daughter, were given the task of guiding the paths of the sun and the moon,

Left: Lord Mulciber the Deathless.

Above: Charm showing the Nameless One.

Below: Roroc, guardian of the Great Inland Sea of Fumoria.

and Noth gave birth to the seasons to produce order in nature."

Many Gibblin folktales recall the ancient ways of earth and forest. This is the story of the Destiny Stone:

"Once a gardener named Bath Boggard dreamed that he was alone in a desert. He came upon a tree surrounded by a circle of tall stones and from the tree hung a golden apple. As he gazed at it, he heard a voice say:

In The Lay of Bath Boggard, *a magic tree is said to guard the Destiny Stone.*

'Hearken, stranger. This is a magic tree, chosen by Golmeth to protect the Destiny Stone. This gem, more beautiful than the stars, more powerful than the wind, holds the fate of the good king. Only when the stone is revealed may he return to his ancient lands.

'On the ground before you, you will find three pebbles. With them, you may try three times to knock the golden apple from its bough. If you succeed, the spell will be broken. Each time you fail, part of you will be turned to stone. Miss three times, and you shall be as these standing stones.'

Trembling, Bath threw once. His legs turned to stone. He missed again, and was petrified to his arms. The third time, he shut his eyes, threw the pebble, and knocked the apple to the ground. There was a peal of thunder and Bath felt the earth quake beneath his feet. Pain shot through his body as he was plunged into spiraling darkness.

Bath awoke to find himself cradled in the mossy roots of the tree. In the stillness, a beam of light broke through the canopy of leaves, and Bath, holding a heavy crystal gem, was caught in its radiant glow.

The leaves shivered as a voice proclaimed: 'Now shall my destiny be fulfilled!' "

Bath Boggard.

Opposite: The dreaded Assizes.

Laws

Mark well the words carved on every prison door in Fumoria, and on many in the Three Counties besides. In this land, Ids impose Mulciber's law, which binds and constricts all daily activity. Who can avoid coming into conflict with it?

Before the arrival of the Ids, folk in the Three Counties had always managed their own affairs. Gibblin hearth-courts, made up of lore-masters and presided over by a swane, settled disputes and discussed local matters. But when the Urgs came through Badland Gap early in the First Treglath (F.T.) and took to plundering the countryside, Gibblin groups called Runners were formed and were empowered by the hearth-courts to deal with the lawless Urgs.

On the orders of the Fu'athan, everyday life quickly fell under the influence of the Ids and the Supreme Court at Diz. Most Urgs adapted to the new order, delighted that the tables were turned against the Gibblin Runners, and many now joined the militia. New Fumorian laws were announced daily, and included, to Gibblin dismay, not only offenses like tax evasion but also "crimes" such as singing in public, herb gathering, mushroom picking, or anything else an officious Urg cared to question. Penalties ranged from cleaning an Id's boots to

Prisoners incarcerated in the dank dungeons of the Assizes are rarely permitted to see the light of day.

getting ducked in the nearest pond, but the worst punishment of all was to be sent to the Assizes, the prison at Hogs Bromley.

For Gibblins, this is the ultimate punishment, since it usually means transportation and banishment. And in case you think prisons are much the same everywhere, let me tell you a few things about the Assizes. For a start, it is the largest building in the Three Counties. Work on it began in the year 674 of the Second Treglath, and when it was completed seven years later, locals were imprisoned in it to test the effectiveness of the new dungeons.

To this day it remains a grim place, and Gibblins whisper the names of its gates and towers with dread: Felons Gate, where prisoners pass in but never out; the Gates of Doom that beckon those condemned to transportation; Beggars Gate, which leads to the underground labyrinth of verminous dungeons occupied by the poorest prisoners; Maggots Tower, named after the Urg prisoner who spent 46 years inside it; and the Keephouse, infested with bats that constantly invade the jailers' living quarters to steal their food and shower them with droppings.

The Urg jailers themselves are infamous for their cruelty and greed, and prisoners are expected to pay for their board, which means they must find money for food, as well as admission and other "fees."

But take heart, dear traveler, and be pleased to learn that in the long years since the end of the Fu'ath Period, the Supreme Court has turned its gaze elsewhere. Secretly the Gibblins have begun to return to their old ways, though the threat of the Assizes and much injustice remains.

Despite the thickness of its walls, many daring and occasionally mysterious escapes have been made from the Assizes. Are these strange marks on the dungeon walls clues to the keys of freedom?

Travel and Transport

Those who excel in traveling leave no wheeltracks.
GIBBLIN PROVERB

"Leave the Assizes and go far" is a saying in the Three Counties and is wise advice to follow, whether you pass through the Gates of Doom or escape through a hole in the wall. Certainly the first way needs no map, for it is the straight road into exile; but the fugitive must be wary, for journeys can be hazardous.

There are no broad highways or paved roads in the Three Counties, merely a network of greater and lesser tracks that crisscross the countryside. During the Fu'ath Period, many of the Gibblin signposts along these routes were destroyed or defaced by Ids and Urgs on orders from Diz and were soon replaced with signs bearing names that enforced the Fumorian highway code. In later years most of these signs were mysteriously replaced, in turn, by the old carved stones that had long been hidden in Gibblin barns and sheds. But many routes are not marked at all, making maps essential for the prudent traveler.

Most folk get about the Three Counties by foot. Gibblins also use boats, and a few have even been known to take to the sky in balloons—an adventure I should certainly not like to try myself! As a rule, except when visiting distant relatives, most Gibblins do not wander far from home.

For longer journeys or for hauling goods, Gibblins use Nags. Strong and sure-footed, Nags pull carts and wagons and can negotiate narrow paths with heavy loads on their backs.

Id palanquins with their Urg bearers.

Urgs, being naturally restless creatures, travel swiftly on their long bent legs and can cover great distances speedily. Ids, on the other hand, dislike walking and hardly use their feet at all. They prefer palanquins, seats borne on poles carried by Urg bearers, who can often be seen lurching along the streets of Ratley or Scrotty Codfield. Imagine the scenes of confusion when the Urgs' customary rudeness, coupled with their passengers' impatience, leads to upset and spillage!

Gibblins enjoy the journeys they make. They honor the natural paths of the landscape, and from ancient times have practiced a system for setting out travel routes. This tradition, also used for situating buildings and planting crops, is known as *Bath'shi,* "the way of wind and water."

Urg boots are strong and well ventilated, with iron hobnails to traverse rough terrain.

The Bedes, the Bath'shi lore-masters, are able to trace the lines of the earth force and concentrate it into energy for growth, directing it toward crops and community centers. Roads can be seen on some of these lines, while others run invisibly across the countryside, their course marked by waystones, hilltops, and trees. Many Gibblins believe that these secret paths, known in folklore as Greenways, provide a means of communication or escape in times of danger.

The *Malbigon* says that the Greenways were first traced out by Elmeth and Noth to help them guide the sun and the moon through the seasons, but of the stones and signs that link a network of secret paths and underground tunnels it says nothing.

A Bede's compass is set with rings divided into segments and is marked with strange letters and symbols.

Opposite: Confrontation between an Urg and a laden Nag.

Topography, Towns, and Villages

Do you know the land where the green tree grows?
In shining leaves a golden apple glows.
THE LAY OF BATH BOGGARD

Ratley

Warty Orton

The Old Mine

To the Gibblins who discovered it, the hidden land on the southern border of the Domain of Maldemon was a refuge from the world of shadows. Remembering the distant beginnings of our three tribes, they called it the Three Counties and settled beside the tumbling streams and heather moors of the Bluffs and Distant Hills. Farther south, they tilled the rich farmland of Scumcrust Vale, their cottages of mellow stone nestling in the shadows of Darkling Wood, and to the south the fens of Green Mere became fringed with Gibblin hamlets. Then, around the year 650 of the First Treglath, a bad year for our people, Urgs marched through Badland Gap to roam the country and disturb the peace.

Let me show you a map of our ancient land and some of the places to visit—or avoid. If you look for the market town of Gibbards, you will see a ruin, now grass-covered, that Urgs reckon is the fort where Foulpiece, one of their most famous generals, made his last stand against the renegade Urg Fatback the Ghastly.

Also of interest to the curious traveler is the large, round barrow not far from Seething Priory, known as Belly Hill. Halfway up stands a tall stone believed to have wonderful powers. On certain nights it is said to glow like fire, looking much like the entrance to a well-lit hall. Many locals claim to have heard music or to have seen folk moving within.

Almost at the very center of the Three Counties lies the ancient town of Ratley. It stands at the confluence of the Scumcrust and Seething rivers, and is the Ratley Hundreds' chief market town. In the Fu'ath Period it was renamed Malzibar, capital of

Hobbs End

Gibbards

Long Balding

Scumcrust Vale

the Chase of Mulciber. Nearby Ratley Bagford is home to the Pigdoom family, who have long been Gibblins of note in the area.

To the northwest, nestling between the arms of the rivers Ooze and Mudd, are the famous cheese-making villages of the Distant Hills: Bilston, Stenchford, and Toad-in-the-Hole.

Farther south, the highlands known as the Blackdoom Hills form a natural barrier to the harsh winds that blow from the Desolation of Orcus. Sheltered by these hills is the chief town of the Scrotty Hundreds, Scrotty Codfield, which is less agricultural than other places in the Three Counties due to the minerals and ore that are mined in the hills. In fact, the area between Scrotty Codfield and Brum leads the way in bellows technology and experimental plumbing.

At the southwestern corner of the Three Counties, the hills finally dissolve into the fens and swamps of Green Mere. This is the source of the River Scumcrust, and borders the edge of a treacherous wilderness known as the Reeks. Now look to where Festerbridge straddles the Scumcrust at its meeting place with the rushing Dankwater. This is a friendly, bustling port, though downriver a solitary quay is sometimes the scene of grim activity. For here is the departure point of the infamous Prison Boat, in which convicts from the Assizes begin their journey into exile.

To the east lies Darkling Wood, vast and mysterious. Despite its dangers, Urgs often roam through it, and Gibblins put up the shutters when they hear the sound of their approach. The south-eastern corner, though, is a different matter: a queer place with ancient trees, where paths are said to shift mysteriously. This is the Old Forest, and Urgs do their best to avoid it.

Close to Darkling Wood lies the village of Deep Ditchford, noted for the nearby Old Mine, once the most important gold mine in the region.

Lastly, a word about holes in the ground, mysterious shafts that are not linked to traditional mineworkings and are found throughout the Three Counties. Most are of unknown depth and extremely dangerous, so keep your eyes open—and beware!

Bilston

Brum

Festerbridge

Scrotty Codfield

River Ooze

Brimstone

Scrotts Bottom

Badland Gap

Overleaf: Map of the Three Counties.

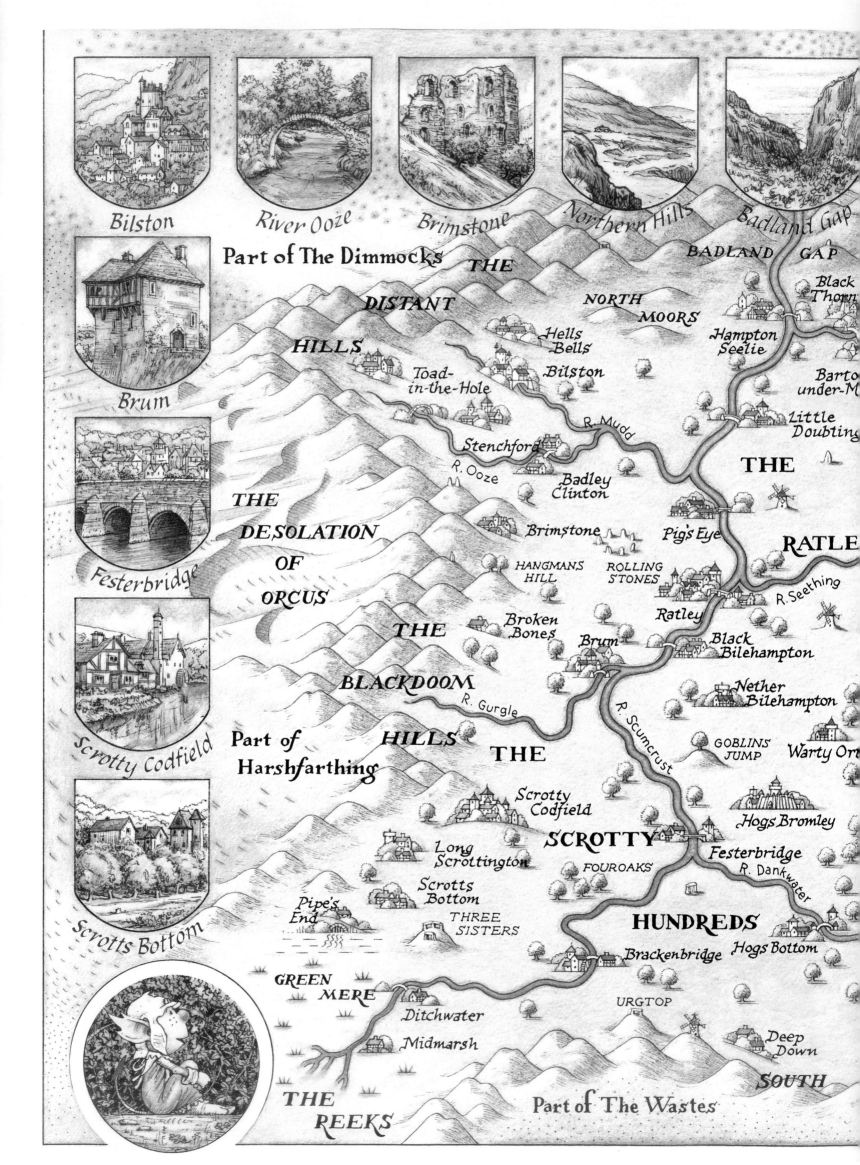

Bilston

River Ooze

Brimstone

Northern Hills

Badland Gap

Brum

Festerbridge

Scrotty Codfield

Scrotts Bottom

Part of The Dimmocks

THE
DISTANT
HILLS

THE
DESOLATION
OF
ORCUS

THE

BLACKDOOM

Part of
Harshfarthing

HILLS

THE REEKS

GREEN MERE

NORTH
MOORS

BADLAND GAP

Black
Thorn

Hampton
Seelie

Barton
under-M

Little
Doubting

THE

RATLE

Hells
Bells

Bilston

Toad-
in-the-Hole

R. Mudd

Stenchford

R. Ooze

Badley
Clinton

Brimstone

Pig's Eye

HANGMANS
HILL

ROLLING
STONES

Broken
Bones

Ratley

Brum

Black
Bilehampton

R. Gurgle

R. Seething

R. Scumcrust

Nether
Bilehampton

GOBLINS
JUMP

Warty Or

THE

SCROTTY

Scrotty
Codfield

Long
Scrottington

FOUROAKS

Hogs Bromley

Festerbridge

R. Dankwater

Scrotts
Bottom

Pipe's
End

THREE
SISTERS

HUNDREDS

Brackenbridge

Hogs Bottom

Ditchwater

Midmarsh

URGTOP

Deep
Down

SOUTH

Part of The Wastes

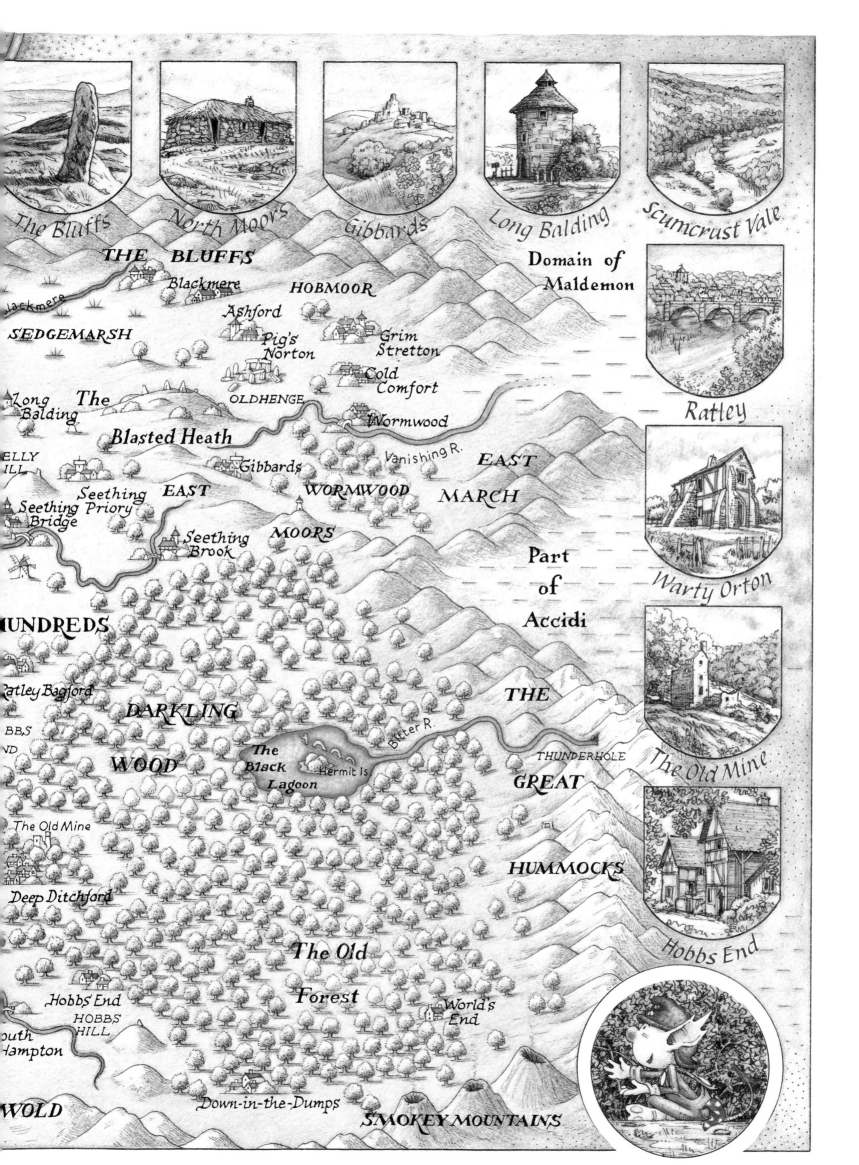

The Bluffs

North Moors

Gibbards

Long Balding

Scumcrust Vale

THE BLUFFS

Blackmere

HOBMOOR

Domain of
Maldemon

Ratley

SEDGEMARSH

Ashford

Pig's
Norton

Grim
Stretton

Blackmere

Cold
Comfort

OLDHENGE

Long
Balding

The

Wormwood

Warty Orton

Blasted Heath

EAST

ELLY
ILL

Gibbards

EAST

WORMWOOD

MARCH

Seething

Seething Priory

Bridge

Seething
Brook

MOORS

Part
of
Accidi

Vanishing R.

The Old Mine

HUNDREDS

DARKLING

Ratley Bagford

BB,S
ND

WOOD

The
Black
Lagoon

Hermit Is

Bitter R.

THUNDERHOLE

THE

GREAT

The Old Mine

HUMMOCKS

Deep Ditchford

Hobbs End

The Old
Forest

Hobbs End

HOBBS
HILL

World's
End

outh
ampton

WOLD

Down-in-the-Dumps

SMOKEY MOUNTAINS

Gibblin Dwellings

*Whoever builds his house on the back of a thunder-lizard
has no close neighbors.*

GIBBLIN PROVERB

On the heather-clad hills, the stone circles left by the Three Counties' mysterious early inhabitants speak of ancient times. Here, too, we find the tumbledown cottages of the first Gibblin settlers. Certainly they were a home-loving people, building dwellings of wood and stone, with roofs of slate or thatch. Today the Scumcrust valley is still dotted with welcoming cottages that bear the aspect of days gone by.

The *Malbigon* says that Gibblins brought the craft of building with them to the Three Counties. Their oldest houses are generally long and low, with small windows set in the walls, simple but comfortable inside. By the end of the First Treglath, houses had become taller, with more rooms, and in the thriving market towns many fine red-roofed buildings flanked the winding streets.

Situated on the outskirts of Ratley Bagford, not far from Darkling Wood, Pigdoom Cottage is a typical example of Three Counties architecture. It was built by Mordicus Pigdoom in T.T.1205 and is presently the home of his great-great-grandson, Wilfus, and his family.

Opposite: Caleb Beldragon's tower.

The Family of Muffin Pigdoom

Home is where the hearth is.
WILFUS PIGDOOM, GARDENER

For years, members of the illustrious Pigdoom family of Ratley Bagford have been renowned as gardeners, lore-masters, astronomers, Bedes, and plumbers. From this account by Carbuncle Beldragon comes the story of their beginnings:

"During the Third Treglath, one of their number, Grimaldus Pigdoom of Brum, boasted ten children, a farm, and a large and

The eldest of ten children, Geronimus the Explorer moved to Ratley Bagford from Brum in the year of the Great Winter. In 1110 he married Angelica Blackmould, cousin of the celebrated millers of Brackenbridge.

In T.T. 1148, Tundric Pigdoom left to search for the Destiny Stone. He was never seen again.

Pigdoom Family of Ratley Bagford

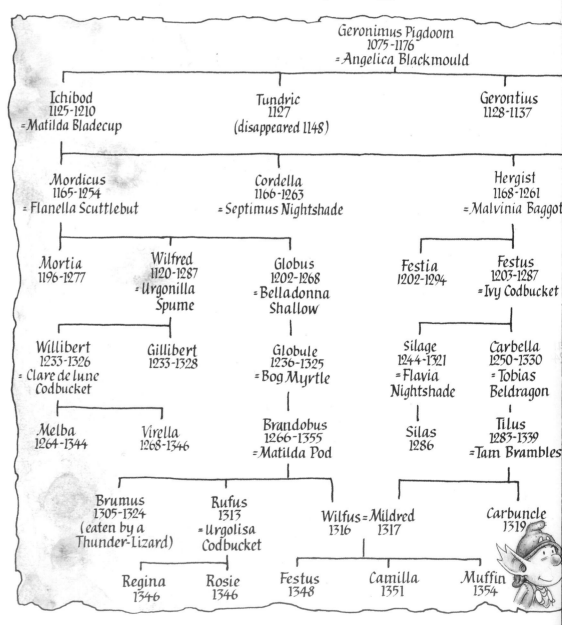

Geronimus Pigdoom
1075-1176
= Angelica Blackmould

Ichibod
1125-1210
= Matilda Bladecup

Tundric
1127
(disappeared 1148)

Gerontius
1128-1137

Mordicus
1165-1254
= Flanella Scuttlebut

Cordella
1166-1263
= Septimus Nightshade

Hergist
1168-1261
= Malvinia Baggot

Mortia
1196-1277

Wilfred
1120-1287
= Urgonilla Spume

Globus
1202-1268
= Belladonna Shallow

Festia
1202-1294

Festus
1203-1287
= Ivy Codbucket

Willibert
1233-1326
= Clare de lune Codbucket

Gillibert
1233-1328

Globule
1236-1325
= Bog Myrtle

Silage
1244-1321
= Flavia Nightshade

Carbella
1250-1330
= Tobias Beldragon

Melba
1264-1344

Virella
1268-1346

Brandobus
1266-1355
= Matilda Pod

Silas
1286

Tilus
1283-1339
= Tam Brambles

Brumus
1305-1324
(eaten by a Thunder-Lizard)

Rufus
1313
= Urgolisa Codbucket

Wilfus = Mildred
1316   1317

Carbuncle
1319

Regina
1346

Rosie
1346

Festus
1348

Camilla
1351

Muffin
1354

comfortable house with frontage on the River Scumcrust. But in the Great Winter of the year 1097, not even the Gibblin ways of cooperation and mutual support could mitigate the disaster.

The Three Counties lay under snow for almost half a year, and many perished in the cold. The crops were frozen in the ground, and in the Great Hunger that followed, four of Grimaldus Pigdoom's children died. It was then that the eldest son, Geronimus, knowing that the little food left was not enough for them all, decided to leave the family hearth. Secretly he slipped away and crossed the frozen river, and for a long time afterward he was believed to have been lost in the snow. But a year of wandering eventually led Geronimus to Ratley Bagford, ready to start a new life and a new Pigdoom generation."

As a local lore-mistress, Gillibert Pigdoom was consulted on every topic from botany to astronomy.

Orcus Pigdoom hated paying taxes. His dislike eventually landed him in the Assizes. He never returned.

Stopcock Foulpipe was a plumber. His tireless enthusiasm earned him the nickname Nonstop.

Matilda Pod, known to all as Grandma Pigdoom, is celebrated in Ratley Bagford as herb-mistress and apothecary.

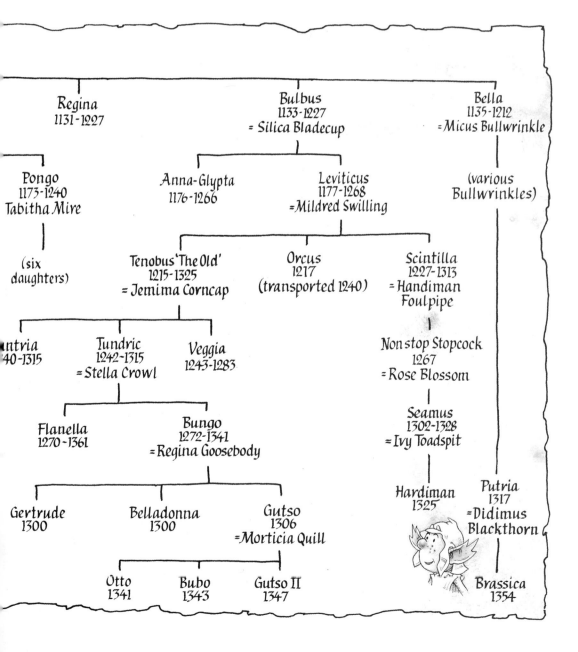

Regina
1131-1227

Bulbus
1133-1227
= Silica Bladecup

Bella
1135-1212
=Micus Bullwrinkle

(various Bullwrinkles)

Pongo
1173-1240
Tabitha Mire

Anna-Glypta
1176-1266

Leviticus
1177-1268
=Mildred Swilling

(six daughters)

Tenobus 'The Old'
1215-1325
= Jemima Corncap

Orcus
1217
(transported 1240)

Scintilla
1227-1313
=Handiman Foulpipe

Nonstop Stopcock
1267
= Rose Blossom

...ntria
...40-1315

Tundric
1242-1315
= Stella Crowl

Veggia
1243-1283

Seamus
1302-1328
= Ivy Toadspit

Flanella
1270-1361

Bungo
1272-1341
=Regina Goosebody

Hardiman
1325

Putria
1317
=Didimus Blackthorn

Gertrude
1300

Belladonna
1300

Gutso
1306
=Morticia Quill

Brassica
1354

Otto
1341

Bubo
1343

Gutso II
1347

Economy, Money, and Taxes

Only a fool knows the price of everything.
WILFUS PIGDOOM, GARDENER

Even a gardener like Wilfus Pigdoom must earn money to pay his taxes. In the Three Counties, taxes are many and varied, and the law is strictly enforced. There are taxes on everything: spring tax, summer tax, winter tax, New Year's tax, seed tax, harvest tax, milk tax, honey tax, leather tax, cotton tax, mushroom tax, toadstool tax, and even tax on tax. Thankfully Gibblins' needs are modest, and, excepting times of flood or famine, we do not want for much.

But modesty means nothing to tyrants, and Lord Mulciber introduced money into the Three Counties to pay the militia and fleece the population. The money value of goods became gold coins called grommets. A Nag was valued at seven grommets, a sack of corn was worth two grommets, and ten grommets might buy a tax collector's smile.

Nowadays, almost everyone uses grommets, though many Gibblins still barter among themselves as a way of avoiding the levy.

In the year 220 of the Second Treglath, the citizens of each county were listed for tax purposes in a document called a *Sku'tag*. Goods and money paid as tribute to Mulciber were recorded separately in the *Codex Malzibar*.

Also at this time, the Gibblin system of weights (called *libers*) was banned by the Id weights-and-measures inspectors, who replaced it with official Fumorian measures. Ids still use Fumorian scales for everything from vegetables to gold. These scales are inscribed with the mark of Mulciber and bear the names of officials who check the weights to stop tax-dodgers from cheating with false measures.

The highborn, of course, do not pay taxes, and Urgs, having no fixed address, are difficult to pin down. But Urgs have always loved gold above all things, hoarding it in caves or

Id weights-and-measures inspector.

burying it in the ground. And, unlike squirrels, they never forget where they have buried their loot.

Banks in the Three Counties are used mainly by Ids. Most Gibblins like to "keep in touch" with their money, preferring to hide it under the bed or the floorboards. The notorious raid on the Bank of Scrotty Codfield in S.T.1877, when the Urg chieftain Anthrax the Bold made off with a dozen sacks of gold, is a popular tale.

The story tells how, after the theft, Anthrax and his gang fell to squabbling, and how during the argument he and his closest companions were slain by the treacherous Urg Leatherlips and his followers, in what was probably a well-prepared coup. After that, Leatherlips and his rebels fled with the booty over the hills into the Desolation of Orcus, the western desert from which no one has ever returned.

Indeed, Wilfus Pigdoom has fallen prey to the greed of Urgs. With each season, roving bands of Urg tax collectors, with or without the authority of their Id masters, comb the Three Counties, banging on doors and demanding immediate payment. On one occasion, the family's entire savings were seized, and only quick thinking saved Wilfus from imprisonment in the deaded Assizes. Truly the tax collectors' motto is "Pay up—or else!"

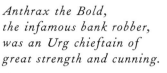

Anthrax the Bold, the infamous bank robber, was an Urg chieftain of great strength and cunning.

More precious than gold are gemstones, coveted by the rich and powerful in Fumoria. Under the law, anyone discovering them must report their find to the authorities, on pain of death.

Employment

It was a golden afternoon,
And Toady's job was done;
So there before his workshop door
He rested in the sun.
TRADITIONAL GIBBLIN SONG

The need for gold to pay taxes leads to work, but for Gibblins, work is a pleasure in itself, being concerned mainly with husbandry and the growing of foodstuffs, building and handicrafts—work where they can see the fruits of their labors.

For the most part, Gibblins do not understand machines more complicated than water-pumps or windmills, though they are skilled at working wood, metal, leather, cloth, and glass. Thus, many Gibblins have flourished as stone carvers, smiths, potters, weavers, carpenters, and cartwrights. Because of their closeness to the earth, Gibblins are also skilled farmers, gardeners, cooks, herbalists, and apothecaries.

Prototype Gibblin threshing machine.

To the surprise of the first Fu'athan arriving in the famed Chase of Mulciber, they found the markets better stocked than many in the Domains. Ids sneered when they observed the Gibblin barter system but recognized that here were workers ripe for taxation. Their lords observed a folk quite unlike the sullen, oppressed people of their own Domains, people who even under the lash would not tolerate the production of shoddy goods.

In the Gibblin markets of the Three Counties the Fu'athan found grains, fruit, and vegetables in abundance, though they were perplexed to find no meats. This is because Gibblins do not kill their animals for food.

They saw blacksmiths, whose eager apprentices cheerfully pumped bellows to fan the flames, and weavers at their looms, making homespun for clothes and furnishings. They witnessed the skills of potters, whose decorated ceramics and pots all reflected a rich and varied tradition.

Because of the quality of their work, Gibblin carpenters and masons were singled out with a covetous eye. They were soon to find themselves in demand on their new lords' flourishing estates.

The highborn themselves did no work, nor do they now, being concerned only with their pastimes. However, one of their obligations under Fumorian law is to raise armies from time to time, and so able-bodied Urgs and Gibblins between the ages of seventeen and twenty-one are required to present themselves for three weekends each year at camps near Brimstone, Nether Bilehampton, Long Scrottington, and Pig's Norton. This edict includes womenfolk. It assumes them all to be as bellicose as female Urgs, so even Gibblin girls are required to attend training.

Urgs with the loudest voices are trained to bark the commands of their Id superiors. The rest become foot soldiers, and a fearsome sight they make.

Gibblins, on the other hand, are not a warlike race, and they have never fought among themselves, though they make good archers, having for the most part been excellent shots with catapults as children.

An Urg trooper carries more than his own weight in armor, weapons, and gear.

Seasons, Festivals, and the Calendar

You'll never see a Yuleth rose,
For many different reasons,
But mainly 'cause it's quite unfit
To grow in chilly seasons.
GIBBLIN NURSERY RHYME

From the progression of the seasons comes the calendar, which was devised by the ancient star-masters to fix the days of celebration and thanksgiving. Gibblins named the seasons after the children of Golmeth's daughter, Noth. Spring is Ostara, summer is called Elmas, Fallas denotes autumn, Winter is Nami.

But when the Ids arrived, the use of the King's Calendar was forbidden, though Gibblin children like Muffin Pigdoom and Brassica Blackthorn are taught it secretly at an early age.

The Gibblin festivals begin in the month of Ianeth, when Gibblins celebrate the rebirth of the year. Special cakes are baked with a bean hidden inside for children to find. Imbolas brings the Festival of Han'driadh, when trees are decked with colored ribbons and Gibblins make New Year wishes. At dawn on the twenty-fourth day of the month of Areth, Bedes greet the sunrise and everyone welcomes the advent of spring. On the first of Samseth, it has long been the custom for Gibblin children to send an unsuspecting adult on a fool's errand. This is known as Hunt the Snook, and I am often that fool! Now the weather begins to improve, and the Festival of Lethe, sometimes called the Feast of Flowers, marks the start of the summer season, when in every village a young girl rides in a flower-bedecked cart led by a boy dressed as the Green Gibblin. Lethe is a popular time for weddings.

Elmas Day, an important time in the Gibblin calendar, marks midsummer and celebrates Elmeth's success in guiding the sun to its solstice. Bonfires are lit on hilltops to salute the bright star

Mrs. Pigdoom baking "sun faces" for Holfas Eve.

Opposite: The Festival of Lethe.

*Alciber shines brightly
in the midnight sky.*

Alciber, visible above the southern horizon in the constellation of the Eagle on this single night of the year. According to legend, Alciber was the grandson of Golmeth and became the first king of ancient Fumoria.

Harvest time brings Holfas Eve, when Gibblins bake small, round loaves, each decorated with a smiling face. These "sun faces," in which the life force of the sun is preserved, are usually kept until the new year. The month of Cereth, when day and night are once more in balance, is the time for the feast of Harvest Thanksgiving. Sammadhain is the festival of summer's end. Upon this eve, travelers should end their journey before sunset for, as the night draws in, Urgs become more numerous and troublesome. Yulthas is the festival of the year's ending, and Yul Eve marks the longest night of the year. Four days later, the Feast of Mithara rings the year complete, and the spirit of the rekindled sun is encouraged with the burning of a great Yul-fire in every Gibblin moot-house.

*Opposite:
The Gibblin calendar.*

The Gibblin Calendar

The ancient Gibblin calendar divides the year into thirteen lunar months, each with twenty-eight days, except Yulath, which has twenty-nine. The names of the months refer to the characteristic weather or growing conditions in that period. Every four years, an extra day is added to the month of Lemnas, making a year of 366 days, a Leap Year. This day is celebrated by a special feast of thanksgiving to honor the Green Lady. The Gibblin days of the week are: Gomak, Turak, Wentak, Storak, Fretak, Nothak, and Elmak. The week begins on Gomak.

Country Lore

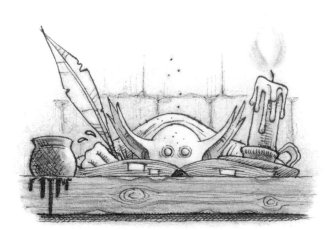

Sing buttercups and mushrooms,
Dance for each delight!
As larks that fly
In clear blue skies,
Or frogs that croak at night!
Cry moonshine and starshine!
O praise the wind and rain,
For the grass that grows
Between your toes,
When sunshine's out again!
GIBBLIN NURSERY RHYME

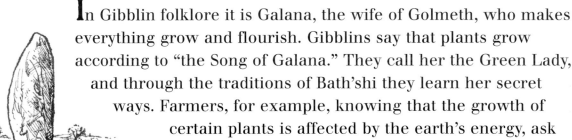

Gibblins believe that the ancient standing stones found throughout the Three Counties have magical significance.

In Gibblin folklore it is Galana, the wife of Golmeth, who makes everything grow and flourish. Gibblins say that plants grow according to "the Song of Galana." They call her the Green Lady, and through the traditions of Bath'shi they learn her secret ways. Farmers, for example, knowing that the growth of certain plants is affected by the earth's energy, ask the Bedes to help them with their cultivation. The Bedes do this by directing and harmonizing the earth force, sometimes using standing stones left by the vanished ancient peoples to help them. In fact, there is a strong belief that it is bad luck to disturb standing stones or stone circles, and that animals may become ill, crops may fail, or even foul weather conditions may result if a site is disturbed.

All Gibblins are expert gardeners. Throughout their lives they acquire a vast knowledge of country lore and the ways of Galana. Trees, they believe, possess *Han'driadh*, or "shining spirit." In *The Lay of Bath Boggard*, it is told how Bath spoke with the Han'driadh of the apple tree in his quest to release the Destiny Stone.

But Gibblins also know that Han'driadh and the power of the Green Lady can be spoiled and depleted. Many are the stories of how Mulciber set his evil against Galana when the Malbigon stone was lost: how, by his ferocious edicts and the evocations of his shadow-makers, the monuments of the ancient ones were destroyed, disrupting the rhythm of the earth force. How forests were felled and rivers were dammed, so that once-temperate lands became dry and burning deserts, and Fumoria was blighted. How the great tree in the center of Diz, known for

time beyond memory as the King's Oak (so tall and mighty that not even Mulciber's strongest axmen could fell it) became choked with corrupted energy, withered and died.

Only in the Three Counties are the old ways preserved. To this end, every year on Elmas Eve, Gibblin lore-masters meet to elect the twelve wisest among them as Guardians to oversee local affairs. Of these, one is also chosen as Guide or Chief—known as the Green Gibblin—whose identity becomes a closely guarded secret.

The Green Gibblin represents an ancient figure in legend called Samseth, who was the youngest son of Ostara, Noth's daughter. Samseth knew the uses of every plant, herb, and flower, and as the keeper of the wild wood, he was entrusted by Ostara to tend the tree guarding the Destiny Stone. Samseth gives his name to the fourth month of the secret Gibblin calendar, and, hidden by ornamental foliage, his carved face peers down from many buildings. He is also found on many objects, stones, and trees as a reminder to Gibblins of their heritage and the ways of the Green Lady.

Below: The Green Gibblin is often used to decorate doorways and arches.

Bottom: Wilfus Pigdoom tends his garden at Pigdoom Cottage.

Education and Writing

A was an archer, as fat as a hog;
B was a bogle, who fell off a log.
C was a cuckoo, who sat in his place;
D was a dodo, with egg on his face.
FROM A GIBBLIN NURSERY RHYME

L ong ago, Gibblins spoke a language developed from the speech of the peoples of Ancient Fumoria. In the period known as the Golden Age, this language developed two distinct forms: High Fumorian, used at the royal court for ceremonial purposes; and everyday speech, known paradoxically as King's Speech. But under Mulciber, King's Speech was suppressed and supplanted by Official Fumorian. However, as with many forbidden things, King's Speech continued to be whispered in secret, so that when Gibblins settled in the Three Counties, the language was spoken freely once more.

Here it has become the delightful Gibblin speech of today. Certainly it contrasts with the brittle chatter of Ids, or the old-fashioned High Fumorian still spoken by the highborn. Urgs, too, have retained their own degenerate form of the old tongue, though it has become very ugly indeed. Most Urgs have harsh voices, and I can assure you that red-blooded Urgish jars on non-Urg ears!

As for writing, it seems that the old High Fumorian scripts of the *Malbigon* were devised for magical purposes. Certainly they are of great antiquity, though their exact origin may never be known.

In the Three Counties, two written languages exist: the letters of King's Speech, called Bard, and the characters of Official Fumorian. Bard is a development of the alphabet proscribed in Fumoria when King's Speech was banned. Originally it was written with brush or pen, but the destruction of all writing

All schools are regularly inspected by Id officials, who insist that children learn their Fumorian letters at an early age.

materials led to its modification as a scratched or incised cypher. Against all odds, Bard survived among Gibblins in exile who brought it to the Three Counties. Here, to their surprise, they found it similar in many ways to the writing that appears on the standing stones of the region.

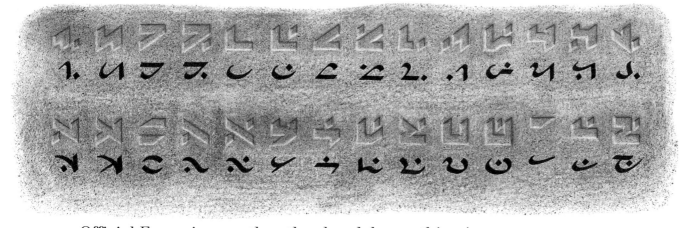

Official Fumorian, on the other hand, has nothing in common with anything, but when it arrived with the Fu'athan, its hard-edged cubic form soon defaced every sign and public building in the land. The cursive form is still used in the documents and accounts of Ids, and schools in the Three Counties are obliged to teach its alphabet.

Fumorian cubic and cursive scripts.

Gibblin education is concerned mainly with the ways of nature, and practically begins in the cradle. Formal teaching starts when children between the ages of eight and fourteen attend school to learn their letters and numbers and enough Fumorian law to keep them out of trouble. Most schools are small, with a single teacher, and all are subject to examination by Ids who comprise the District Inspectorate.

Gibblin Bard.

Id children are quite a mystery—in fact, I have never seen any—but I am told that young Ids are sent to special academies for their education. A few Ids are sent to schools outside the Three Counties, but only the brightest are sent to Diz.

Urgs have no formal education. Most are illiterate, though they are able to count gold coins and figure out complicated betting odds rather quickly!

Illness and Medicine

For blisters, bruises, spots, or boils,
Mix frogseye, nettle, and essential oils;
Apply the balm to ease the pain,
And soon you'll feel as right as rain.
A GIBBLIN PHARMACOPŒIA

It is told in the *Malbigon* that when the Great Pox swept across Fumoria from Bel-Zemoth in the north, carrying off without distinction the children of the highborn as well as Ids and Urgs of lower class, it was an apothecary from the Three Counties who first discovered a cure. Every Gibblin has a rudimentary knowledge of the medicinal uses of plants, and there is also extensive use of snakebite therapy, leeches, acupuncture, and dowsing. Also, Gibblins have long realized the value of certain minerals and stones, knowing that many are very active and can absorb or emit energy.

Urgs know enough to chew hogsbane for belly-ache, rub worm's balm onto blisters, and drink an infusion of gripeweed and mustard for trapped wind. They also claim some skill in the use of stones.

Ids are secretive about their ills, though they tend to get headaches and melancholia, and, in common with Urgs, find halitosis and boils a problem.

In the Three Counties, the Gibblin herb-masters and apothecaries are renowned for their ability. So while I give my rheumatic knees a rub, let me describe some common ills and their cures.

The healing power of onions is well known. Urgs, for example (and I don't fancy this myself), use a hot boiled onion to relieve the pain of ear-ache. They also believe

Gripeweed has many uses in the Three Counties.

An ancient Urg remedy for earache.

that onions absorb infection, and, during a recent dragon-pox epidemic at Grim Stretton, a peeled onion was hung at the entrance to an Urg encampment. No one in the camp caught the disease, and when the onion was taken down, it was found to be black and soggy. "The pox had flown straight into it," claimed the chieftain.

Lumbago and similar complaints, sometimes called "the screws," commonly afflict those living in damp places. Around Green Mere, folk believe that a garter made from the skin of a mud eel and worn just below the knee prevents the screws from rising higher. Elsewhere, snakeskin is worn similarly against cramp.

Bruise ointments are made of yellow spleenwort, toadflax, urgsbalm, and thistles, all stirred into hog's lard, while the creamy juice of slugsedge, a charm against sunstroke, is often used as a soothing balm for beestings or burns.

For "harvester's wrist," apothecary Matilda Pod prescribes a blisterine and scabious poultice. For fractures, the glutinous root of talsiney, known as knitbone, is grated for plaster and sets as hard as stone.

Eyesweet and frogseye have long been used as ingredients in an eye lotion for tired eyes. Less well known for indigestion is the use of water from a blacksmith's bosh, or cooling trough. This is highly effective against the bloat. Blacksmiths are also credited with the power to stop bleeding. And prudent housekeepers take care to leave a few cobwebs undisturbed, for if bound over a cut, they are believed to help clot the blood.

Matilda Pod, author of A Gibblin Pharmacopœia.

Lastly, wart-charming is a mysterious and essential skill.

Most healers include a substantial number of Ids among their patients, all desperate to be relieved of the unsightly lumps on their heads. One popular remedy is to cut notches on a stick to correspond with the number of warts to be cured. The stick is then buried till it rots, taking the warts with it. Some charmers claim the power to cure warts by rubbing them with their fingers, and are said to be skilled at "shaking hands with warts." Others chant, "Oaken tree, oaken tree, will you take these warts from me?"

Indeed there are many charms, but of them all, those for wart-healing remain the most baffling.

Beasts and Other Hazards

Brave lads are we,
Who roam the glades of Darkling Wood,
Avoiding thunder-lizards,
Though half our tribe ends up inside
A thunder-lizard's gizzards!
FROM *THE FLIGHT OF GENERAL TOADFIRE,*
AN URG LEGEND

You should know there are still worse ills in the Three Counties to be avoided. There are two kinds, the first ill being the malignant creatures that inhabit the secret places of forest, swamp, heath, and cave.

Most fearsome of these is the dreaded thunder-lizard, king of Darkling Wood and consumer of hapless Urgs and others who disturb it. This monster grows to thirteen meters and spends much of its time asleep, but when roused its bite is deadly—and one bite is usually all it takes! Just as deadly are the swiftfoot lizards, reptiles with keen eyes and mouthfuls of razor-sharp teeth. They hunt in packs, running upright on muscular legs, and are capable of great bursts of speed.

And keep your eyes open for scissorbacks, scaly creatures with razor-like tails that lurk in the undergrowth; and the venomous spider-frogs, with poisonous spit and eight legs-a-leaping, that inhabit the tops of trees. Beware the spring-jackets, jumping mud crabs with sharp pincers and a leap of fifteen meters; and the blargs that roam the Blasted Heath on moonless nights.

Poisonous spider-frog.

The second group of ills is no less deadly than the first, but they are easier to avoid. These are the environmental hazards: for example, the famous hailstorm with stones as big as thunder-lizards' eggs that once fell from a clear sky over Little Snogging; or the great electrical storm that swept up from the Wastes and razed half the trees on the southern border.

More recently, an alarming earth tremor shook the entire Three Counties from Badland Gap to

Pipes End. It felled many old trees in
Darkling Wood and dislodged slates from
the roof of the Keephouse at the Assizes.

Also to be avoided are those mysterious
holes that open without warning upon heath
and hillside and swallow whole herds of Nags;
the shifting bogs of Green Mere; the scalding
springs of the Wastes; and the uncharted quicksands
beyond the Dimmocks.

A mysterious hole.

Leavetaking

Golmeth is the father of heaven and earth;
Galana is the mother of all creatures.
These two are one,
Different only in name as they issue forth.
Being one they are called mysteries,
Gateway to the many secret paths.
THE *MALBIGON*

Who knows where a falling star may land? In the *Malbigon*, it says that the flame that burns in every star burns in a Gibblin's heart. Certainly, from the tops of the hills their cascading trails are delightful to see, even on the shortest night. Enjoy them and wonder at the bounty of the heavens! In the Three Counties, the fun will last from dusk till dawn, when even Urgs may seem more well-mannered and Ids may unbend a little.

At such times a single star may rise and fall to remind us that a good king once ruled— and will one day rule again. For travelers in the Three Counties, it is a time to remember. So ponder on these things, for I must say a reluctant good-bye until our next meeting. . . .

Farewell!

Caleb Beldragon

Opposite: The secret Gibblin map that shows the labyrinth.

Here are set forth
The hidden treasures of the earth,
Where the stars of heaven
May be found in the hills.

The earth contains
Its own stars,
To which Golmeth gave the brightest
Its qualities and powers.

Discover by turns the earth's delight,
Follow her green ways.
But first be sure the time is right;
If you find yourself in doubt,
Listen closely to the old stories.

The Malbigon *reveals, to those who can see, things that are and were, or yet may be. One of its most intriguing passages tells of a place where hidden paths lead to a labyrinth. At the very heart of the labyrinth lies a fabulous treasure. The* Malbigon *says there is only one correct way in. Which is it?*